is going places!

date

Going Places

Written by Peter H. Reynolds and Paul A. Reynolds

Illustrated by Peter H. Reynolds

A
atheneum

Atheneum Books for Young Readers
New York   London   Toronto   Sydney   New Delhi

Rafael had been waiting
all year long for the
Going Places contest,
a chance to build a go-cart,
race it . . . and win.

When their Teacher announced,
"Who would like the first kit?"
Rafael's hand shot up.

The rest of the class watched enviously as Rafael walked back to his seat with a kit.

Mrs. Chanda assured them, "Don't worry—
you'll all be getting one . . .

. . . and they're all EXACTLY alike."

The kit came with a set of precise instructions. That made Rafael happy. He was very good at following directions.

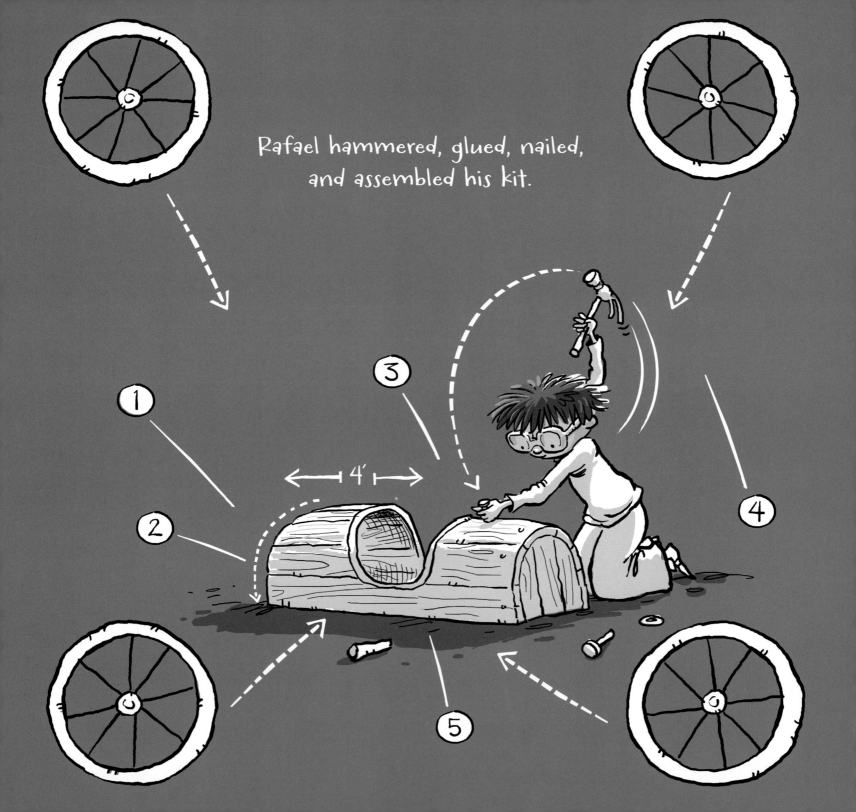

His go-cart looked just like the one in the directions.
He was feeling quite proud.

Rafael wondered
how his classmate Maya was doing.
She lived right next door.

He peered over the fence.
"Hey, Maya, you haven't even started?!"

Maya didn't respond. She was so intent on watching the bird in front of her, and quickly sketching it, that she didn't even notice Rafael.

Then she just put down her pencil
and stared at the bird dreamily.

Rafael shrugged—and let her be.

The next morning
Rafael checked back in
to see how Maya was doing.

"Wow, what is that?" he asked.

Maya grinned.
"You like it?"

Rafael responded slowly, "Yeeeaah—extremely cool.
But, uh, Maya, there's just one little problem.
That's not a go-cart."

Maya smiled. "Who said it HAD to be a go-cart?"

Rafael was confused. The set of instructions inside the box were for a GO-CART. But then again, they didn't say it HAD to be a go-cart. He looked again at Maya's contraption. After a moment, he grinned.

"I get it. Hey, Maya, I really want to win this race. The instructions never said we couldn't team up either!"

And so they did, working late into the evening.

The next day everyone gathered for the big race.
Each go-cart was a perfect replica of the other.

Except one.

One of the kids laughed. "Looks like you had trouble with the **Going Places** instructions. You're going places all right—you're GOING to lose!"

Maya and Rafael didn't even have time to respond because the announcer's big, boomy voice called out,

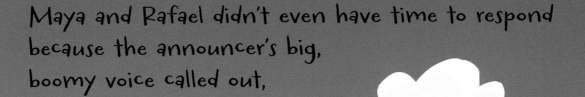

ATTENTION, RACERS!
START YOUR ENGINES!
4...3...2...1...

A buzzer sounded.

"And they're off!"

While all the other go-carts disappeared in a cloud of dust, Maya just sat there in their motionless vehicle. Rafael shouted over the roar of engines and cheering crowds. "Maya! What are we waiting for?"

"No worries, Rafael!" Maya answered.
"Flaps down, throttle up!"

And now THEY took off—off into the air!

The other contestants
looked up in amazement.

Maya and Rafael hovered and then sped past them all.

Before long, Maya and Rafael coasted across the finish line to the cheers of the waiting crowd.

They kept rolling clear across the race grounds. Maya slammed the brakes, stopping just short of the lake at the edge of the school field.

Rafael noticed a startled frog leap from a lily pad and dive into the water. He raised his eyebrow and looked at Maya. She smiled.

"Rafael, are you thinking what I'm thinking . . . ?"

Rafael just nodded.

To all the great thinkers
who have gone above and beyond.

And especially to Dan LeClerc, our tenth-grade
social studies teacher, who dared us to have original ideas.
—Peter and Paul

$\mathcal{A}$
atheneum

ATHENEUM BOOKS FOR YOUNG READERS
An imprint of Simon & Schuster Children's Publishing Division
1230 Avenue of the Americas, New York, New York 10020
Text copyright © 2014 by Peter H. Reynolds and Paul A. Reynolds
Illustrations copyright © 2014 by Peter H. Reynolds
For information about special discounts for bulk purchases, please contact Simon & Schuster Special Sales
at 1-866-506-1949 or business@simonandschuster.com.
The Simon & Schuster Speakers Bureau can bring authors to your live event. For more information or to book an event,
contact the Simon & Schuster Speakers Bureau at 1-866-248-3049 or visit our website at www.simonspeakers.com.
Design by Ann Bobco
The text for this book is set in Carrotflower.
The illustrations for this book are rendered digitally.
Manufactured in China
0415 SCP
4 6 8 10 9 7 5
Library of Congress Cataloging-in-Publication Data
Reynolds, Peter H., 1961– author, illustrator.
Going places / illustrated by Peter H. Reynolds ; written by Peter H. Reynolds & Paul A. Reynolds. — 1st ed.
p. cm
Summary: Rafael has looked forward to the Going Places contest and builds his go-cart from a kit in record time,
but his neighbor, Maya, has a much more interesting and creative idea for her entry and Rafael decides to help.
ISBN 978-1-4424-6608-1
ISBN 978-1-4424-6609-8 (eBook)
[1. Creative ability—Fiction. 2. Karting—Fiction. 3. Contests—Fiction.] I. Reynolds, Paul A. II. Title.
PZ7.R337645Goi 2014
[E]—dc23
2012051351